First Edition: 5th March, 2020

Title: The Mystery of Miracles.

Published by Ma Manasa Publishing Company India.

Mumbai, Maharashtra, India.

# Dedication

The book is dedicated to the cause of humanity, peace, prosperity and happiness.

The characters of this novel are all imaginary. If those resembles to anyone that is a coincidence and the author cannot be held responsible for that.

# Preface

There are both uniformity and diversity among human beings. The first uniformity is that in every human body there is flow of blood. The second uniformity is the constituent organs of the human body. The diversities are lot more in number than uniformities. Among uniformities and diversities one thing is ordained to keep in mind of all human beings is that they are one, one human community. As being the one human community, they have established their supremacy among all other creatures of this earth, then, the responsibility to show harmony and bring peace in this world maintaining the beauty of the earth is theirs. Like uniformity the diversity should also be worked for the total well-being of the community as a whole. The diversity is being used in various fields as the weapon of non-cooperation, resulting in injury to the peace and harmony. Being the human, the humanity should prevail among all human community members. Every human should follow the ethics and morality. Peace is the indication of prevailing these two heavenly attributes in the human society. In the world peace is not established meaning that ethics and morality are not reining. Literature is working through the ages to bring consciousness among humans to develop their best attributes for peace prosperity and happiness in all human societies. The purpose of this book is also to send message to the society to give priority for the peace prosperity and happiness of the community as whole.

The Author.

5th of March, 2020.

Glasgow, United Kingdom

A dreadful sound resurfaced from the sky and passes through, tearing the horizon from one end to the other. The sound is so mighty that it looks eight thunders happen at a time in the sky and struck the ground. Mallikarjuna wake up and see an enormous dazzling light nearby and feels the immense heat. Rubbed his eyes, only to check whether what he is seeing is real or he is dreaming. It's true. Without doubt it's true, he murmured. "The fusion reaction, as happens in sun, is happening here and I am so close", he shouts and start running towards the fire. He has no fear in his mind now and does not care the fire. He starts running towards the fire losing himself in joy and jumps on the fire with extreme glad. Instantly, a big bubble emerges from the fire keeping Mallikarjuna within. The bubble starts running upwards at light's speed. Mallikarjuna is still in his best elated mood. From inside the bubble Mallikarjuna starts seeing that live pictures are floating on the sky. He watches the pictures very minutely. He identifies his father and mother with a baby on his mother's lap. "Who may be the baby", he questioned himself. Within no time he realises it is definitely he. Because he is the only child of his parents. Sequentially, since his birth all his life start floating live on the sky like a film. He is very excited to see his life in such a lively condition. Initially, he sees the live film of his life astonishingly. At a later part he surprised why this is happening and how am I running upwards so fast being within the bubble. He asks himself, "where am I going and how, where is my destination". The live pictures of his life still continuing on the sky. Forgetting everything he goes about to see the live floating pictures on the sky. As the pictures are advancing towards his life he is becoming more curious to see the next one. Without any hunger or nature's call his eyes and mind are fix on the live floating pictures of his life.

Suddenly, his bubble come very near to the moon and the live moments of his touching the moon appears on the sky. He realises how easy he is reached to the moon now but when he set out for the journey to the moon that was a big mission and a very challenging and prestigious project. Mallikarjuna settles on, quietly, to see the pictures of his life floating on the sky.

At one point with his extreme surprise he sees the sky is end and only the fire surrounding the whole horizon is only burning. "Here again the fusion", he exalts. His bubble penetrates the gigantic fire without any burn and he feels no heat. He notices lots of big fires are burning and there are gaps too. His bubble passes through the gaps between the burning fires. He has no doubt in his mind now, that this is certainly the sun and the fusion reactions within it. The gaps between the fires are definitely the solar scars. So, he shouted with all his energy, "I have reached to my coveted destination I have cherished for the whole of my life". But how this impossible becomes possible so easily, he surprised and shouted again, "who will answer my question". At this moment, the burning fires disappear and a never seen shooting light appears bringing within him a kind of joy which he never felt and which in no cost can be sacrificed. The sounds coming waving to him from within the heavenly light answering his questions. He is asking more and more questions and the light is answering. The question answer session continues. This question answer session reveals what is the truth and the mystery behind all miracles. Before knowing what is the truth we peep behind who is Mallikarjuna and how this happens to him.

Mallikarjuna is a scientist and does research in physical science. He is also a noble laurate in physical science for his outstanding contribution to the field of physical science. He has successfully performed his moon mission. His inventions have benefited the human kind a lot. He is bachelor and a man who follows the ethics strongly throughout in his life. After reaching his puberty he never touched any women and never intended too. Throughout his life he has two ultimate targets. One is to reach to the sun and the other is to reach to the centre of the earth. Both are impossible at present state of the science. To make the impossible possible he has worked a lot and longed for reaching the two destinations. He is currently living in south India along with his four other celibate noble laurate scientists hailing from various parts of the world. The four others are Alan from England, Ronald from America, Christopher from Brazil and Julius from Africa. The moral characters of all are the same and that is why they can live happily together. The house currently they live in is called the Power House by the local people. Because they can make solutions to every problem of the local people. They are revered and really loved by the local people for their magnanimity and humanity. They have earned a lot of money through their inventions and discoveries and few of them have inherited huge money from their forefathers. They spend lots of money for the benevolent work of the local people. They jointly own a small ship and a helicopter which they use for their expedition and local journeys. The power house is also equipped with all elements for research and innovation in any discipline. They have decided to spend the rest of their life together and in Power House only.

Mallikarjuna has designed and built a vehicle with an intension to reach to the centre of the earth. The vehicle he has named as Mighty Digger. This mighty digger shapes like elongated screw as like the penetration part of earth digger. It has three upper covers and an inbuilt engine below all three covers. The upper most cover is fitted with moving teethes made of chromium. The middle cover is fitted with small propellers. The propellers are made of chromium but they are covered by a very unusual material of human navel. Mallikarjuna has spent a lot of money for procuring honestly the human navels, people of India throw in the river after burning the dead bodies. This part of the human body cannot be burnt by fire or electric and is also not rotten in any environment. The lower cover is the same as that of upper cover. Beneath these three covers the engines and sitting rooms are fitted. The upper three covers can move keeping the engine and sitting rooms stationary. The cooling arrangement inside the sitting room is also meticulously done. Inside the vehicle four persons can sit. One at the front, at the driver's seat, two at the middle and one at the rear. The vehicle is not tested but its estimated speed of earth penetration is within the range of 50-60 kilometre per hour. The shape and movement of the mighty digger can be well imagined when its mechanisms to penetrate earth are more clearly defined. The mighty digger can penetrate the earth and speed past the magma level but it can also go down to the deep of the water once its upper most cover is made to burst for destroying it. The vehicle rests on the ground horizontally on a stand. Once it is started the stand helps to make the vehicle erect vertically and separated automatically from the vehicle. The vehicle then starts penetrating the earth. It throws off the mud and stones to a certain particular height so that they fall on the ground and not on its created hole. It is intentionally so designed. Because when it starts from an open ground the generated whole remains hollow for a certain height at which it can throws off the particles. When it goes deep down further the opening of the whole covers but it has already gone deep to that particular length at which it can throws off particles keeping the certain length vacant between its extreme rear and the deposition layer of its cut particles at the distance it is throwing off the particles. Thus, anywhere in the deep of the earth a certain hollow height is maintained. The particles throw off by the mighty digger are crumbled and porous and it help passes the flow of the wind the vehicle creates.

The screw ridges of the mighty digger are fitted with teeth wheel which spins on electromagnetic environment. As the teeth wheel spins a particular fluid sprinkles on them to keep them cool. The upper cover can penetrate the muddy and stony substances of the earth. But once it will reach to the magma, the lava level underneath the earth, this cover will be melted. To make it safe, once it reaches to the magma level, the first cover is consciously burst off for its destruction instantly and the middle cover to start propelling. Mallikarjuna has researched a lot to create this middle cover. There is only one substance in the world which is not melted by the magma. It is the navel of the human body. In the middle cover, above the metal there is a cover of navels. The navels are also pasted with a special organic fluid invented by Mallikarjuna. The middle cover is made like a propeller to pass through the melted lava. Once the magma layer is reached the upper most cover is intentionally made to burst instantly to maintain the hollow of the height to pass through the vehicle to wards the centre of the earth. The mighty digger cannot change its direction. The particular point it starts in the earth's surface it reappears at the diametrically opposite point of the earth surface. The lower most cover of the mighty digger is similar to upper most cover. Once the magma layer is finished the middle cover is also intentionally burst to destroy instantly and activated the lower most cover to cut the earth materials to penetrate. Upon this mechanism the mighty digger is built upon. Very recently Mallikarjuna had called in a press conference to display the mighty digger to the journalists and expressed his intention of venturing into the expedition to the centre of the earth with this mighty digger any moment. Thousands of requests have poured in from the scientists' community and from the various national governments not to take that venture before ensuring 100 percent security, the expedition is called off temporary. Another reason for not setting for the expedition is that the mighty digger has four seats only and they are five. They are now in such a bond of love among one another that no one wants to leave the other in such a risky venture. The mighty digger is resting on the power house ground under a shade to be tested on the right occasion.

Mallikarjuna and his power house friends have successfully made Antarctica expedition with their beloved small ship named MV Lovey. During that expedition Mallikarjuna was noticed a small island not occupied by any organic lives. The island is situated at the south end on the Indian ocean. They christened the newly discovered island as Lovely Island. He had intended to visit that islands any time in the near future very soon. A week before this miraculous incident he had set out to reach this island at night without accompanying any of his power house friends. He reached the island just at twilight of the day. He was gleefully moving here and there for few hours and becoming tired he was a little bit sleepy. The sky breaking sound wakes him up. What happened after that is the ongoing event. After his departure from power house until now his friends are frantically searching to find out him. To see the result of question answer session with the unseen light we are now returning to the sun where Mallikarjuna is interacting.

The answer start waving down to him resonating in the atmosphere, it is your strong desire, your honest will and benevolent work for the mankind have altogether brought to you here. He question's the light what is truth and what is illusion, who controls the universe, is the universe static or dynamic, if the universe is dynamic then how can it be explained, if the universe is static then why we see it active, why am I not burnt to ashes when I have reached to the sun. The answers started waving down to his ears. The universe is infinite and static. It is one and the one is the one light and no others. This one in the form of light is the truth. It is one and undivided. It is the original. It is not created. It was, it is and it will. It has infinite power but it is inactive. Infinite is always infinite. Whatever is taken from infinite it is still infinite. The visible active world looks huge to the humankind but if it is deducted from the infinite universe, the universe is still infinite. The active dynamic world can not be said to be a part of the infinite universe, because then the universe can be measurable. If universe is measurable then the question is what is there after it's end. The universe has no inner or outer part. If a circle is drawn in the universe, it creates a limit and something within and outside the circle can be indicated. The active world is a closed line within the universe and is controlled by a will power. The will power is existing everywhere within the closed line. The will power can take any amount of power from the infinite power of the universe to transform it to any form. Whatever infinite could give out it is still remaining infinite. Minus the active world or the closed line the universe is still infinite with infinite power. The will power is also original and not created but it is not infinite. It has the taking ability from the infinite. The will power is only active within its closed line. The closed line can move anywhere within the infinite universe and it is dynamic. The position of the active dynamic world within the universe is beyond the determination of any particular location because the universe is infinite. The universe or the truth is always static and infinite. The will power is the one who is realising the truth always. Beyond the boundary of its activity it is witnessing the one and only static infinite light called the truth. Nothing can be separated from the one and only light then what is remaining within the closed line is also truth. The second existence except the one and only light is the will power within a closed line within the universe. The will power is the controller of the dynamic world. This will power is the god and whole static universe is the Brahma as mentioned in Hindu mythology. Whether the will power within the closed line is remaining within the universe or not, the universe is infinite always. The will power thus cannot affect or impact the truth and cannot also separate the active world from the universe.

The will power creates only the illusions. The will power has a finite area within the closed line whatever vast that may be. When it transforms the form of the truth in any one limited area, except it none other is witnessing or realising that. But when it transforms the form of the truth in any second limited area in the same form or the other as of the first and one or both of them can witness or realise the other one or both of them, then both are feeling the existence of a second object. In both the areas ultimately, the truth is remaining but the will power has transformed the truth to a different form. The will power transforms the truth to a different form for a limited period and gives it a boundary. That limited period may be for ages. But it does not keep it for perpetuity. It keeps changing one form to other. What is created by the will power is to be destroyed or transformed to other form at some point of time. The illusion is therefore, which has appeared from the truth through the will of the will power and to be destroyed or to be transformed to other form in some point of time or other, that is, which has a certain span of existence in any form other than that of the truth. The will power knows that it is only transforming the real form of the truth to other form and that is also not for perpetuity. It keeps the desire hidden within the transformed object to return to its true form. The will power is existing everywhere within its boundary. In every transformed object it is existing and every transformed object has a will power which actually the one who has transformed it. The will power when voluntarily confined in the transformed illusion obeys the command of the illusion in which way it will move. Either going to return to its true form as soon as possible or continue the re-transformation process to delay the path of returning to the true form. Truth is the one and manifests only in the form of light which is one. Then how is the movement of the illusions created by the will power can be explained? Movement is the displacement of any object from one place or area to other, as is conceptualised in the human civilisation. If the will power creates any illusion or object transforming the truth and wishes it reappear in other area in the same form it can do so and the other illusions then realises that the illusion or object is moving. All objects which are existing in the active world are illusions. When objects are moving they are actually re-appearing in one position to other within the boundary of the active world. The will power is also the one who is the idea maker of the active world. It creates uncountable ideas of illusion creation and weave them in perfect fashion. It can remain idle keeping the truth in its real form within its boundaries. But it feels happy creating and weaving ideas of illusion making, transforming the truth. This is the mystery of the universe and the miracles created by the will power by making the illusion of a dynamic active world. When it wants the will power can re-transform all the illusions to the truth and then there will be no active world. The will power then moves its boundary in a different position within the universe. In a different position the idea of a different active world is formulated by the will power. This reality can explain every happening of the active world and the power of the controller or the god of doing anything it wants.

When the will power moved its boundary in its current position before time immemorial it had fancied how it will start its new active world and gradually go forward with the weaved ideas. This active world is going along with the sequence of the ideas the will power has crafted them at the outset. The complexity and enormity of will power's ideas and their sequential knitting are not imaginable totally to its transformed illusions. Time has reached to give certain understandable preaching to the humankind, one of the illusions of its kind of the will power, for their guidance to reaching to the truth. You feel no heat while you are here because you have been transformed, transformed from human body to human soul and you are protected by the will power.

Having heard all these utterings, Mallikarjuna further hears, "Mr Mallikarjuna, you have still a desire to fulfil and that is to reach to the centre of the earth. You can be easily reached there because you have reached so close to the will power. You have now immense power and any impossible can be made possible by you if you wish only. Human beings are far away from the truth and it will take long for them to reach to me. You can pray for three wishes which will be fulfilled by me for all human beings in the earth to reach to me and after that you will be mingled with me".

Mallikarjuna says, "My first wish is that there will be wisdom of light in the earth and all evils are wiped away. My second wish is that there will be equality among human beings in all respect and my third wish is that I can answer rightly of any question asked to me. Please also tell me who are you".

Mallikarjuna then hears, "all your wishes will be fulfilled when you will desire and I myself am the will power, the controller of the dynamic world or the god, any of one name or in all of them you can prefer to say".

Hearing this X becomes so joyful that he wants to burst out of the bubble. The bubble then starts coming down towards the earth very fast. It looks like a huge star glittering and reflecting light. It reaches the earth at night and submerged into the Indian ocean. It comes down to the ocean bed and start penetrating the earth very smoothly. It stops at the centre of the earth and settles there.

As soon as it stops at the centre of the earth a tremor is felt through out the globe. All science centres of the world start investigating the cause of the tremor and the epicentre of the tremor. Mallikarjuna's power house friends also, among concerns of finding out Mallikarjuna, start investigating the cause of the tremor. In the next day, all science centres give the statement to the press unanimously that the epicentre of the tremor is the centre of the earth itself. Mallikarjuna's powerhouse friends also reached to the same conclusion. But they are very worried about missing Mallikarjuna. One cargo ship was returning from South Africa to India and the caption of the ship watched that glittering light. He is very surprised and think that any meteor is sinking in the ocean. He also thinks of any imminent danger and cautioned all his colleagues narrating the incident. He gives press statement in the next day coming ashore about the star like glittering substance, reflecting light sunk in the Indian ocean. Few believed his statement but most are not. But his power house friends guess Mallikarjuna has done something new invention and they still continue searching the whereabout of Mallikarjuna. The captain of the ship also stated that he has seen the MV Lovely floating in the Indian ocean near the new discovered island. Mallikarjuna's power house friends become very concerned. They seek government's help and anxiously waiting for his return.

At this point of time a beeping signal starts to come from the giant television room of the research building of the power house. When they all four reached there they see the giant television is automatically opening. After a few seconds of blurring the image of Mallikarjuna, standing within the bubble surfaced. They all exclaimed, "ooh! where are you?" With their extreme excitement Mallikarjuna replies, "I am at the moment at the centre of the earth". "How do you have reached there? they all questioned together. "That's an awesome story", Mallikarjuna replies. Mallikarjuna then says, "I have a lot of things to say you". Then he starts saying.

A wisdom of light will flood a part of the earth that will wipe out all evils. The light will start flooding the earth when I signal that to happen and it will cover any one-degree part of the earth up and down from the centre. No human being can prevent or control that light and no one can see that directly. What will happen where the light will flood will only be reflected in this giant television. You can broadcast the scene to the whole world from here. You can make a press conference and make arrangement for worldwide broadcasting of the new happenings. You are all famous and trustworthy scientists of the world and include my name also. Governments and people throughout the world will believe you. You can rest assure that it must happen. Spread this news to all science centres of the world as soon as possible. This is a first of its kind miracle happening in the earth since its birth.  My appearance in this way looks miracle to you but its not at all miracle, I have now immense power and can do anything good which you think impossible. If people want to see me in this position allow them and also the scientists who want to investigate. All of you jump start on your duty and I am giving you reasonable time to serve this news to the world and arrange for broadcasting. Whenever you need me I will appear on this giant television before you.

All of Mallikarjuna's friend called a press conference immediately and the news spread to the world in lightening speed. Many rumours also started to spread. Mixed reaction of truth and false about the happening and sarcastic remarks from high and low start flowing here and there. All his friends make arrangements for broadcasting of the happenings worldwide. Even in disbelief anybody dares to ignore the incident because of the world-wide high reputation and popularity of the Mallikarjuna and his power house friends. They all give green signal to go ahead to Mallikarjuna. Mallikarjuna then give the exact time of 24 hours from now when the miracle will start to happen. That news also spread throughout the world immediately.

Count down starts and all world stop working and breathlessly waiting before their television screens to see the never seen. Finally, the moment came. The giant television screen in power house opens up and the whole world watch that Mallikarjuna is standing within a babble. He just says, "the wisdom of light you come at one-degree part of the earth now". A part of the world appears on the screen. The part appears is as normal as other part of the world. Then starts the flood of light. Ahead of light are coming millions of black giant hands which are holding the human beings in tight grip and throwing them with mighty power. Nothing is seen where they are reaching. Everything on the earth, like the houses, the hills and the mountains and seas are bursting off and flood of light engulfing them. It is only the soothing white light, something like deep white fog is only can be seen. A new earth starts building inside the light. The bubble of Mallikarjuna starts moving through the deep dark and stops suddenly where the light of the bubble illuminated faintly the whole area. It is seen that millions of silhouettes of demons are fighting among themselves. Millions are also lying on the ground and groining. At this moment sound starts waving down from the air and everybody watching the television broadcasting are also hearing that. This is a place where the souls of the demons are confined after their death. Their souls also fight here continuously with one another for ages. When they are unable to fight they start to groin. Their groin continues and nobody of the fighting demons pay any heed to their groining. Few of them get emancipated when any light of this kind as of your's now which all of you are seeing now, penetrates in this world. To fulfil your wish the part of the earth has been inundated with the light of truth and this area has been infected with millions of demons just now. The lying down demons who are groining now will get their emancipation very soon as their time for punishment has been over and they have got the feelings of the light of truth. The rest will continue fighting for ages as they have still their spirit to fight and have not got the feeling of the light of truth. You are now returning to the centre of the earth. The new world on the part of the earth where the truth of light has inundated will now be displayed on the giant television of your power house and the whole world will see that.

The bubble of Mallikarjuna reaches the centre of the earth and the new world where the truth of light inundated starts to emerge at the giant television of the power house. The whole world is astonished by the view of the new world on the light inundated part of the earth. A clean, round and flat earth with green ground surfaced. There is no end of the ground. Soothing white light is illuminating the earth. Lots of young human couple are dancing on the ground, all making exactly the same pose. All couple are top to bottom green coloured and standing side by side on the appeared ground. The man and the woman are the same height and weight. Their body is covered with certain unseen material of green colour but any normal human being can identity who is the man and who is the woman. When they are moving, they are moving in the same direction and in same stepping. Both man and woman have the same sweepings. The green ground is unending and the direction of their movement cannot be identified as front or as back. They stop together and utter something. Then the same food starts to pour in their mouths. The flow of pouring in food stop suddenly and they start to move further. Then came the deep darkness and nothing is seen except the darkness.

Then again appears the bubble and Mallikarjuna says from inside the bubble that the whole earth will be like this after 359 days and in each day one-degree earth will cover from top to bottom. Today is the new moon day and the next transformation will start on the next full moon day. Only 15 days remaining to start the continued process of converting the earth in to this world. Although this may not happen, if two conditions are fulfilled simultaneously. The first is that, all human beings do not want this world and my bubble is burst even second before the start of the new conversion process. Only 15 days' time and if it starts again no one can stop the rest of the earth to convert to this world. The earth will definitely convert to this world and after the second stage conversion starts, I have only one task to complete and then this bubble and I will be no more. The control now on the hands of the people of the earth. Only one opportunity is there to choose between the current world and this new world. But remember all human beings desire not to happen this and my bubble is burst even moment before the second stage conversion starts.

Not a single normal human being misses to see this broadcasting even the child also. The thinking of the earth changes dramatically. Even the hardcore atheists dare to disbelieve. Every normal human being starts thinking what to choose. The world leaders immediately start a video conference among themselves to unanimously decide what to opt for. Within minutes they decide not to allow this world to happen. They start on war footing basis to persuade people not to desire for this new world. The military of every country is asked to opt for continuation of the current world and go to the civil society to convince everyone to opt for the same, by even coercion or intimidation. In the video conference the leaders also agree to make an immediate network of all world scientists and engineers for every second update of the way out to prevent happening this world. The world computer engineers make a mechanism of uploading and displaying on electronic medias, each and every person's thinking about the way out to convince every person not to opt for this new world. The terrorist groups through out the world united within few minutes and unanimously agree that their action world is the current world and in the new world they will be no more existing. So, the continuation of the current world is their only choice. They instruct their armies to prepare for any subversive action any moment to destroy the human beings who do not want this current world. The world starts to see the mighty power of networking and the unity of the human community. The leaders address to the terrorist organisations to come open to save the world without fear. The dedicated military generals of all countries vehemently oppose the proposals of world leaders of seeking terrorists help. Immediately the terrorist leaders assure the world leaders to terrorise every people to opt for the current world. Their armies come open to the society to terrorise all people. Very quickly one of the world leaders assess the consequences of applying nuclear weapon to kill all the humans and save a particular island. Whatever be the use of nuclear weapons in the world that island will not be affected. He appeals to all leaders to assemble together and flee fur away to that island taking as much resources as possible and kill the rest of the humans with nuclear weapons. Then only they will remain in the world and opt for it continuation and it will continue. There is no risk that anyone cane opt for the reverse. The terrorist group being frightened at this proposal of that world leader take ransom of all the world leaders immediately for their own safety. If all people desire not to opt for the new world and the current world will continue, then they will control the current world. The idea come from network forum to apply one to one option. A is the option of continuing this current world and B is the option of go for the new world. A opting persons will ask their immediate near persons about their options and if there is opposite either persuade him or her or call the help groups. Help groups are the national army of the country, terrorist groups and groups formed by civilians to save the earth from converting to the new world. One suggestion displays on the electronic media that even if all normal persons agree to continue the current world then also it can not be stopped because mentally imbalanced persons and child could not be convinced and the condition is that all persons should desire not to go for the new world. The army and terrorist groups then started to drug out the innocent child who playfully are saying that they want the new world and also the mentally imbalanced and brain dead who cannot speak properly. The child and the handicapped persons are being assembled in several points for mass killing by detonative. The furious parents and relatives revolted and a civil war is about to start at every corner of the globe. The military of every country and terrorists' groups are ordered to execute total annihilation of the civil society of entire globe. The world is witnessing the ruthlessness and cruelty of the human beings for selfishness. The execution groups even prepared to kill their own children and the near and dear ones. The rich and powerful become very happy because what they wanted is automatically happening. The power house friends of Mallikarjuna are extremely shocked with the disaster of the earth and desire to contact Mallikarjuna and he appears. They ask Mallikarjuna whether the mentally imbalanced and children could not make an exception. Mallikarjuna answers as they are not mature their desire does not have any impact. The answer of Mallikarjuna is broadcasted live. The whole human community in one voice cheered we don't want the new world. We want to live in our present world. The terrorist organisations start to take credit of the victory and declare, once the bubble is bursted, they will take control of the world and rule as they want. They will fulfil their dream and thanked Mallikarjuna for making such a situation for them. All these happened within a very short span.

Then came the attack on the power house. Even if all existing people in the world do not desire the new world then also the second condition of bursting the bubble of Mallikarjuna remains. The bubble of Mallikarjuna must be bursted. The four power house friends are forced to start the expedition to the centre of the earth with the mighty digger to burst off the bubble of Mallikarjuna. Other scientists who are available nearby are forcefully brought in from various parts of the world very quickly to establish a tracking of the mighty digger and taking its live pictures as it progresses inside the earth till it hits and burst the bubble of Mallikarjuna. That mechanism is easily done by other scientists. Cameras inside the mighty digger are fitted and arrangements are made to take the inside live pictures of the mighty digger. Live pictures of Mallikarjuna and his bubble are continuously displaying on the giant television of the power house. Everybody is assured that when the mighty digger will hit the bubble of Mallikarjuna, then no live picture of bubble of him will not appear. Other scientists present at the power house discover the mechanism to ensure that the mighty digger reaches the centre of the earth. Mr. Alan sit on the driver's seat of the mighty digger and switched on it to start. The stand of the mighty digger vertically placed it, facing its front to the earth. The outer cell of the mighty digger starts to spin at the speed expected by Mallikarjuna. The stand of the mighty digger departs off from it and it goes down to the earth gashing out the muds vertically to the sky as predicted by Mallikarjuna. The track down of the mighty digger also starts to appear in a separate television screen set up by the other scientists. The broad casting of the same starts to every houses of the world. Now only one thing to watch by the world's human community when and how the mighty digger reaches to the bubble of Mallikarjuna and burst it off. The mighty digger is penetrating deep and deeper towards the centre of the earth. The other scientists have an apprehension of how the mighty digger will work on the magma level. The power house friends are continuously charting with Mallikarjuna and as they are continuously charting that is displaying on the giant television of the power house simultaneously the movement of the mighty digger is also broadcasting. The mighty digger is speeding very fast as was predicted. The scientists calculating it is going past at a speed of more than 200 kms per hour. The mighty digger starts well before the beginning of the second stage of new miracle world. The speed of the mighty digger suggests that the showdown will happen within 12 hours. All persons of the world are in front of the television and watching spell bound. The other scientists establish a special signalling system for identifying when the mighty digger is reaching in the magma level. That signal starts to beep and the scientists watch that mighty digger is intact in magma level and speeding as fast as in earth level. The other scientists were doubtful about the crossing of the mighty digger of the magma layer. As the power house friends are approaching near and near to the centre of the earth all are becoming very exalted. The friends are extremely eager to meet Mallikarjuna and so also he. The present scientists at power house give commentary that mighty digger is very near to the bubble of Mallikarjuna, so everyone expands their eye lids to see their most desirable in life. Within a second the giant television of power house displays that mighty digger hits the bubble of Mallikarjuna and it's all end in giant television. The mighty digger is also vanished and no connections are established. They joy of the world reach to the extreme level ever from the moment of the creation of the earth.

But that joy is only momentary. Fight starts between the army of each country and the terrorists. The terrorists are spread every corner. They take ransom of all common people. The military of all country are helpless now. The military generals remain consciously silent only to make a way out. The world come direct under the grip of the terrorists. They had their long-term plan that has been successful today. The military of every country is showing the loyalty to them only to keep the common people unharmed and there is no way. The terrorist captured the world's administration. Their new world king is declared whose coronation day is selected on the next full moon day. All of their group admitted that before coronation also they are loyal to their new king. The new king orders to execute all head of states on the very next day including the power aspirants on the second line. The heads of states begged for their life but that is not granted by the terrorists. They did their first terror duty by executing all the heads of states in a single day and in the very next day the power aspirants of the second line. The price of selfishness is paid in real worth by the new administrators now. All except the new administrators and their supporters are repenting for their decision to opting for this present world.

Nobody can open their moth in fear of the new administrators. Tears and agony are the all-time companion of majority of the people of the world now. The atmosphere of lull is everywhere. Childs are almost numbed. In inner mind of all affecters are praying for the good time. Time will not wait for none. It is only passing by. The next full moon day reaches. The new king of the world will now be sworn in tonight. The moment is fixed. Order comes from him for compulsory rejoicing of all at the moment of swearing in and his men are watching all. Even in hardest of infighting within the mind, all have to laugh and rejoice. This day is the toughest day in the history of human kind. Countdown of the swearing in moment starts. All the world is watching and showing artificial joy. Only a second to go, the new king is going to adorn the chair. At the moment earthquake starts. The new king falls down on the ground. The earthquake stopps. All are surprised at the surfacing of the scene. Before everybody of the world, Mallikarjuna within the bubble and all four of his power house friends encircling him appear. The mighty digger is also seen standing at a little distance.

Mallikarjuna starts talking. All human beings of the world are now seeing and hearing me. No need to broadcast me through scientific instruments. Unity is the most important thing the world now needs. The unity should be for a great cause. The united power always challenges the evil power. You show some unity to challenge the heavenly power and welcome the evil power. The result is as eternal as you are getting now. All of you are problem ridden in some way or the other. None of you can say that no grief has come to you ever in your life. You can not stop sorrow to come to your life. You are dependent on others, dependent on heavenly power. The horizon is always open to you still you cannot see it in real sense. You can not feel it. You can not try to be it. You are only concentrated within your physical limit. Your body. A perishable material. Hardly you think who controls the perishable. Who is the real, the perishable or the controller of perishable? Within the perishable what most can you expect? The whole of the earth or now what you can extend to even the moon and with further stretched of your demands, one or few other planets. But if you think about the controller within the perishable you can get the sky, where all the materials you aspire for are creating, existing for a certain period and then destroying. You can create and enjoy what you want. But now, even acquiring the whole of the earth or even some planets what else you can give to your perishable. Only certain materials which are negligible in proportion to your possession. Then what is the real benefit of vast possession. You are giving more and more pain to your perishable body. At the moment your own controller within your body is leaving the perishable, you or the perishable, only long for further existence of your own controller. I am meaning your soul, which you definitely understand at the moment. But that does not happen. A wonderful world is displayed before you where there is no pain to your body, no hurt by anybody, only joy, happiness and peace are reigning there. There is no existence of evil in this world. A call is given to you to unite for this world of joy, peace and happiness. Unity for a great cause and be united with the all-powerful. You welcome the evil and get the punishment. You challenge the all-powerful and get repented. You never think 700 million cannot unitedly welcome the evil at a time and challenge the heavenly power. One or two might be there, who are fearless and strict to the ethics, whatever be the consequences. You are so engrossed in devil that you were about to kill even the innocent en-mass. Your call is the loser. The real worth of humanity is the loser. The earth will convert in to the wonderful world in the next 359 days from now. You still have one more opportunity just to make your call the winner. Be bold to the great cause unitedly, whatever be the apparent circumstances may try to terrorise. Whoever will remain for the rest of the days try to make a call for the unity for peace happiness and prosperity. The message is that the evil will never win. Always resist them. Let the real sense of humanity to win. Now its time the wonderful world will take shape within the earth and all can see without any television.

A part of the earth merge in to the wonderful world. The existing demons reached to their demon world. The wonderful world is increased by certain number of inhabitants. The fortunate start their new life. Now I am signalling the second stage conversion of the earth to the new wonderful world and all of you who are escaped today just watch that. I am just going to fulfil my next task and nobody can see me anymore.

After the second stage conversion of the earth starts all four power house friends circled Mallikarjuna and say, "we have few questions to ask you". "Right", replied Mallikarjuna, "And I am given the power to give their right answers".

"So, lets now start". They uttered together.

The question answer session then starts. Before knowing the questions and answers we can see the impact of the Mallikarjuna's speech to the human world.

The speech of Mallikarjuna makes all good people courageous and enterprising. Everybody has become certain about their fate in the near future. The common people automatically dare to challenge the terrorists and start fighting with them. The army still now silent in apprehension of harm to civilians start to show their valiance and vigour. They are the group who do not care about death and torture. They are dedicated to give their life for the cause of the country. They fight in war to give peace to the country. They are the harbinger of peace. That sense arose to them and they fight tooth and nail with the terrorists. The terrorists began to find hideout again but still some devil people are helping them. Good people are trying their best to give the remaining world for the remaining days a happy and peaceful existence. Bad are always bad. Even knowing that days are numbered for all, they still finding some ways to make wealth and enjoy at the cost of injury to others. Fight between good and bad continued. World becomes calm to a certain extent. Sensible people developed some good senses. The ever-increasing tendency of majority of people to earn more and more money for more and more self-enjoyment and accumulation for the future for self and own family reduced to a great extent. People start to work for the great cause. To give the food to the hungry, to make home for homeless, to nurse the sick, to give the child more amusement, to produce more food in the field, and other of these types of benevolent jobs.

A group, most of them are journalist, start to investigate why people who are suffering the most, like fatal disease attacked people and destitute people still opted for this terrible world over the wonderful world. They start to question a lot of people of those categories. They got the answer which is surprising. They see that whatever be the bad conditions of people they always aspire for what they desire in their life. Even if it is not possible in their life span they keep hoping that their next of keen can fulfilled it. Parents want their unfulfilled desires will be fulfilled by their off springs. Even one who does not have any near one desires that somebody else will do that but that should happen in some day or other. Because of various unfulfilled desires which are only possible to be fulfilled in the current world, people who have lost all still opted for the current world of numerous sufferings instead of the beautiful wonderful world.

All of the four friends put the question before Mallikarjuna, “Why this wonderful world is created and how?

Mallikarjuna starts answering.

You will come to know how it is created, if I present before you the scenario of how I reached to the sun and what happened there. The scenario starts to appear before the power house friends of Mallikarjuna. Just after the scenario disappear then again Mallikarjuna starts answering why this wonderful world is created. This is a lesion to the human beings of the earth. After its resurfacing, the earth has gone for overhaul restructuring millions of time. The present stage of the earth is the most recent. And like me you all know that this stage is got to be somewhat stabilized millions of year ago. The main lessons the central controller wants to send out to the human beings are to control the boasting of dominance and superiority, throwing away the laziness and cruelty, and cultivate ethics and morality. You have already learnt that at the very beginning of creating this dynamic world the controller had the set the ideas and their sequencing. So, after a relatively stable condition the flora and fauna are created. Which are recognised as life in this earth. In reality there is no definition of death. The end of life or destruction or disappearance of any substance are mere transformation. The flora and fauna are destined to survive on material substances on the earth and its atmosphere. The ideas of how they will survive are also sequentially knitted by the controller. The sequential knitting of the controller, we, the humans, describe as evolution. You can now understand every creature or material substances are the manifestation of the controller himself. But to give the feelings that they are separate entity an invisible limitation line is drawn. Within this invisible limitation line, the controller's will power is active. Still, as a limitation line is drawn the controller has created a will of choice to drive the will power in the direction it wants. One is the front direction and the other is the back direction. The front direction is the will of the entity to be mingle with the will of the central controller. The back is the going away from the mingling path. The entity which is strongly willing to mingle with the central controller will mingle with the controller sooner than the entity willing in the back direction. The back-direction selectee entity will ultimately recourse the path of front direction. But after a longer time than the front direction selectee. There is not time concept to the central controller. The meaning of back direction is the becoming of obscure of the will of the central controller within the entity. The front direction is the right path and the back direction is the wrong path. When the back direction of the entity or entities go far away the layer of obscurity becomes dark and darker. Then all actions done through the will of the entity are wrong actions. The central controller does some actions to re-direct the will of the entity or a group of entities to turn them to the right path of mingling with it. He does it by appearing in the form of a sage within the human community. Who preaches how to reach to the god and in our current discussion as the controller. Now coming back to the flora and fauna. The flora is straight forward. They just to try to keep the process through which they have created. Once they cannot keep the process to continue they are transformed to other entities. Once their regular process is stop and they start to transform, we then called them as dead. What they left are their next generation. That is called creation and coincides with the will of the controller. The controller limits itself to several parts as form of numerous entities and continue the creation stream. A creation once it is emerged continue to keep its existence, this endeavour of continuance of existence is called the survival process. It is true for all existence even for other material substances barring the flora and fauna. This survival process has led the back direction of will of the fauna. Over the ages human beings have been the controller of flora and other fauna. Superiority and dominance concepts have been embossed within them. The dominance concept has brought in the laziness concept. Displaying the superiority, the dominance has been imposed. Imposition of dominance has influenced the laziness, moving away from ethics and apply cruelty. Let it explain broadly.

Let us take the ages from the grouping of the human beings. They grouped together for survival. One of the group members displaying his superiority among others in strength or intelligence or in other respects becomes the leader of the group and starts to dominate the group. Once his dominance is established he can manage his survival needs without giving his full labour and laziness start to creep in. The concept of king, his dominance superiority and extravagance has started from that period. Dominance superiority and extravagance are all corelated and have charmed majority of human beings. Who are charmed with those attributes and materials, try to reach a position of that, either individually or collectively, even taking recourse to cruelty and renunciating ethics. The back direction of the will of the entities work when their will direct to attain to that position.

The history of civilization of human beings is very long. The history means records. Simply think that if all records and identities of all human beings are withdrawn from the world then what will happen. The human beings who were kings before will also have to search for their food for survival. If controller fix's strong ethics on every human being nobody will claim more than equivalent to his given labour. This is meant to signal that controller has not given any certificate of claim to anybody. All material substances are the individual manifestation of the controller. He or she whatever we can conceive is the creator of everything. This eternal truth almost every human being has forgotten today. Almost everybody is trying to reach the position of superiority, dominance without ethics for extravagance in life. Ethics and morality can only bring peace prosperity and happiness in this world. Ethics is almost vanished in this world and so is peace. Ethics is humanity. Humanity directs the will to touch the will of the controller to reach to the truth. Where is the humanity? Hypocrisy has taken position in place of humanity. Majority of the people in a position to take decision for others or want to gain something from others are hypocrites. Everybody knows hypocrisy is dominant in this world. Still people are becoming hypocrites and even believe hypocrites. Frustrating is the case of displaying boisterous false superiority and dominance claims. Where there are people there are the bragging of superiority and intention of domination by all. Boastful Superiority and dominance competitions are existing in continents, countries, regions, arears, houses, languages, looks of people, colours of people, heights and weight of people, knowledge of people, intelligence of people, expertise of people, wealth of people, way of talking of people, art of people, food intake of people, discipline of people, clothes of people, health of people, diseases of people, history of people, religions of people, casts of the people, genders of people, child birth of people, sports of people, classes of people, attributes of people and nothing left beyond competition. Competition in one to one, one to many, many to many, group(s) to group(s), nation to nation. competition is not for competition's sake.

Competition is associated with hypocrisy, cruelty, ruthlessness and devoid of ethics and morality. Competition is also sometimes unsolicited and hidden and only to inflict harm to other party without any fault or misdoings. Except few sages nobody thinks innumerable superior things are there of what one is boasting of. If all of the above things are withdrawn or make uniform then there is no room for superiority among human beings. The controller has created inequality to see how the human beings can make balance of equality by co-operation among themselves, not by competing without ethics and being cruel and ruthless. The attributes of motherhood, fatherhood and brotherhood are considered now as written in the god's literature, not present in the mundane world. These attributes of motherhood, fatherhood and brotherhood are the examples of front directional movement of the will of the creatures. The central controller has infinite power and can do anything only if his will desires. The wonderful world he has created now falls in his sequence of ideas and nothing new to him. At the very beginning of creating this dynamic world he has thought of this because the picture was clear to him that back direction of will of his creatures or he himself in limiting format, will bring such a stage of dreadful competition only for destruction. In this new world he has not kept any room for competition. Here all human beings are created in equal couple. He has not rule out the concept of creation. Because it is his will that creates and he gets material for his will to play. He has kept the gender in this new world also. Assimilation of two genders creates another. But here the genders are not different entity. They are two in one. What they do, they do together. They are never separated. The only difference in looks between man and woman is only to identify two separate genders and mean that the creation is still existing. All couples are the same look. In no circumstances they will be separated. They are just shown differing physically but their brain is one. So, no couple think different. Whatever they think they all think the same in every moment. They do not have to think for how their life will go on. Whenever they wish for food, they wish all at a time and get that automatically in their mouths. They do not know what food they are getting. They do not have any natures call. They do only two thinks together, wish for food at times and play always of what their central brain or brain of everybody thinks. The light in their world switched off at times and the world becomes dark for their rest and reproduction. Child birth from them and rears but that are behind the curtain. It is the responsibility of the central will. When child attains the same physic as they are, the central will brings them in this world. Their central brain or their individual brain never feels that. In the dark what happens they do not know. They do not have the feelings of how many they are in number. Once again when the light switched on they again start playing and wish for food at times. Nature is absent in this world. The horizon of the green ground is stretched to infinity. The green ground and green colour are meaning the existence of activity. In human sense it means life. This world has no relative direction also, no back, no front, no up or no down. As there is only one brain there is no competition, no cruelty, no hostility in this world. This world is for peace enjoyment and happiness. When all human beings fail to reach by themselves to create peace and happiness, the central will himself creates that in a different way. This is the logic behind the creation of this wonderful world. The controller has infinite power and he can do what he wants. As I said earlier that this idea of creating this new world was sequentially knitted when he thought of creating this dynamic world.

Now Alan asks, “Why the idea of religion introduced in the world and despite the goal of every religion to achieve peace harmony and happiness the humanity never get a peaceful world?”

Answer. One of the world-famous sages once defined religion as the creation of divinity in humanity. Divinity as we so far explained as the front direction of the will of the creature to reach to the will of the controller. The controller is the divine power so far meant by the sages and his will is the act of divinity. What the controller does through his central will is always divine. In his creatures he creates the will and gives the freedom to move the will in both front and back direction. The actions of the back direction of the will moves away from reaching the will of the controller. The actions of the back direction of the will of the creatures are regarded as devil works. The advent of human civilization is the indication of maturity of human brains. With the advance of human civilization the human attributes of dominance, superiority, laziness, cruelty have also started to develop because of the movement of the will of the human beings in back direction. The will of few human beings have also started to move in the front direction and they drive that till they reached to the will of the controller. The deep and prolonged meditation, sacrifice and sufferings they resorted to drive their will to reach to the controller. Once they reached to the will of the controller they come to know the truth. Once they mingle their will to the will of the controller they can do any miracle which other common people can not do. Other people start to see them with reverence. They also noticed that will of the many people are going in the back direction and they can not reach to the will of the controller until change the direction of their will. They introduce certain rules and regulation which can change the direction of the back movement of the will or advance further the front directional will of the creatures. These rules and regulations are called ethics. The followers of these rules and regulations make a group and desire to be identified by the group only. Obviously the group got a name. The name of the group take their root in the human civilization as a religion. One further explanation is necessary. The truth is one and the unending infinite light. Then all the sages when reach to the truth they see the same one and the only. Then the rules and regulations of all religions should be the same. But the introduced rules and regulations of different sages as in enshrined in different religions are differing a little bit. The sages could see the position of the will of all their followers and could measure how far they are in back direction and how far advanced in front direction, on individual to individual basis. Accordingly, they set the necessary common rules and regulations to be followed by all. In various zones of the world this position of the will among the followers was different and accordingly the rules and regulations in different religions have differed. But what ever rules and regulations they follow they can reach to the will of the controller. One set of rules and regulations is called a way of reaching to the god or the controller.

The peace is established when all human beings are following the ethics or the rules and regulation of his or her religion preaches. That is the movement of will of every human being is in the front direction. That may be a rare happening until the whole human community is guiding by a sage who has reached to the truth or touched the will of the controller to be united with him. It may also be possible that the whole human community is divided into several groups and each group is preached by a sage who has reached to the truth. When a group is directly watched by a sage who has reached to the will of the controller, the sage can measure the position of the direction of the will of every individual member and tell him the rules and regulations he or she will follow to direct his or her will in the front. Even if it is not possible for one to change his or her will in the front direction the sage can apply the infinite power he is capable of manoeuvring to change the direction of will of his or her in the front. Every religion has failed to direct the will of every of its member in the front direction for three reasons. First is the absence of the sage who has introduced the original rules and regulation for his or her disciples. Second is the preaching of the rules and regulations by a next person who has not seen the truth but only mentored by the sage who introduced the original rules and regulations. The third is not obeying of the original rules and regulations of the sage of introducing the religion. When the truth witnessing sage transforms his mundane limitation to be united with the controller, the religion of his her introduction, or the rules or regulations or the ethics, are preached by a next person who has not reached to the truth but gotten valuable guidance from the sage, then he fails in measuring the direction of the will of every member of his group and guide them to the need of the moment or even change the back direction of any member with his miracle power. Sometimes even the new preacher modifies or make changes to the original rules and regulations of the religion and as they are not certified by the truth they can not change the back direction or advance further the front direction of the will of the members. The group members even following the rules and regulations of the religion cannot then change their back direction of the will and total ethics are not prevailed within the whole group. Peace is not assured then. The simple rule for every human being is, be human, develop humanity first and then divinity. One who can follow this will see that all original rules and regulations his religion supposedly directed to follow are followed automatically. All sensible people who understand this analogy if adopt humanity is their first religion and follow the set of ethics and also preach to others to follow the religion of humanity above all then peace will be established in the world.

Every human being inherently is religious, that is the desire to unite with the controller is either active or dormant. As the will of the controller is existing in all human beings but being limited within a boundary it is directed to either front or back direction. Religious attributes are exposed for all who are directing their will in front direction but at some point of time the direction of the will definitely change who are presently directing their will in the back direction. The condition of peace is the movement of will of all human beings in the front direction at a time. The humanity being mother of all religions can make that possible.

Ronald asks, “Which is best form of rule, the monarchy or democracy?”

Answer. Monarchy is the best form if you get the best ruler of the region. But the king is not judged as the best among all the rational persons of the region. A judgement is necessary to choose the ruler for getting the best rulings. Until unless a truth witnessing sage tells that who is the best ruler, seeing the future in advance by his miracle power or by the manoeuvring power of the infinite power, the judgement of a person as the best ruler needs a process. Selection process is the best. But the problem in selection process is that all probable capables do not offer themselves available for the job and there is involvement of cost. If from the existing talents who can rule the best of the region somehow does not come to the probable's, then even after selection process with incurring of expenditure the desired result cannot be obtained. The election process of rulers for a region is now given the definition of democracy. In democracy there are two or multiple parties, who sell the ruler claiming to be the best and the common people opts for buying. Democracy is also not uniform in its characteristics. Somewhere a party as a group begs for option from the common people and projects its choice later one. Somewhere, an individual begs for option on behalf of the party. The common characters are involvement of parties and common people. This involvement of the parties is the bad side of the democracy. Two parties or multiple parties who are involved selling ruler to the common people maintain a big cadre to project themselves or to their rulers. Only the winning single party or a group of parties can rule but the opponent other party or the group of parties are not entitled to take part in ruling process. The productivity of the losing party or the group of parties are of no use to the region. The expenditure incurred on this losing group either from the government or from the public directly or by themselves are producing no good and services for consumption of the region and a wasteful expenditure. If that group were involved in other productive process, their produced goods and services were added more to the production quantity and could have enjoyed more by the region. The more the number of parties in the region is involved, the bigger will be the cadre of unproductive people. To reduce this number of unproductive people, the number of parties to be reduced to minimum. In a democracy minimum two parties must be involved. So, two party democracy is the best for any region. The people of the region must be forced to sacrifice that much of expenditure for wasteful purpose to be get ruled. In monarchy if the luck factor clicks, that is the next monarch is the best ruler of the region, then it is the golden opportunity for the people of the region, because no cost is involved then. The monarchy and democracy both have merits and demerits but the best form of rule is when the ruler is following the ethics, be it in monarchy or in democracy.

Now Christopher asks "what is the concept of marriage and does the same gender marriage fits with that?

Answer. The controller has his will power to transform the infinite power of the truth. The controller although creates only illusions by limiting himself within a self-created boundary. All the created illusions are he himself. But still likes creation. Being an illusion creature of the controller, the humans being have a will of creation of facsimile illusions within them. Creation is conceptualised by controller only with unitedness of a man and a woman. And before the stage of being one within two, marriage is an idea sequentially woven by the controller. Hence it is a will of the controller and in the human sense it is the formal permission of him before the stage of creation of facsimile illusions. This is the concept of marriage. Same gender cannot create their facsimile illusions, that is, in human world it is called child. The idea of marriage does not fit with the same gender. It is against the will of the controller and an instance of movement of back direction of the will of the marriage partners.

One clarification is put forwarded in this context. Man and woman get joy and pleasure in the creation process of child. That is the joy of creation. That attracts a man to a woman and vice versa. But the two who will meet together to be united for creation are fixed by the idea of the controller. When the will of both of them moves in the front they get united and enjoy the joy of creation and peace. Those whose meeting idea is not determined by the controller but still united on the movement of back direction, apparently, they feel joy but actually that is not and never get peace. The idea of the society that to meet any one you wish with consent from both and united for the process of creation are not following by ethics and morality.

Now Julius asks, "What is the definition of truth in our mathematics and are we going to the wonderful new world or elsewhere?"

Answer. The mathematical definition of truth is, it is one, only one and infinite. Nothing is above it, nothing is below it. You write 1. Put a line above and below one and write 0 in both above and below. Putting zero above a digit marking by a line does sense nothing but zero below a digit by putting a line signifies infinite. That is the mathematical definition of truth.

We are already transformed, means the human body we were carrying are no more with us. I have been transformed once I have jumped to the fire of fusion reaction in love island. What you are seeing me is an illusion of my body. You all are also illusions. Once you have started the Mighty Digger I have given it the power to penetrate the earth smoothly to bring all of you to me quickly. Being submerged in to the lava you all have been transformed and your human bodies are no more. Now we all are going to be united with the controller and his will be our will. I have given that power by the controller and being my friend, I am uniting all of you with the controller with my power.

All of his power house friends looked each other to inspect and started to feel they are no more human beings. They all become light and mixed with the truth for ever.

www.ingramcontent.com/pod-product-compliance
Lightning Source LLC
Chambersburg PA
CBHW062145160726
48282CB00027B/945
* 9 7 8 8 1 9 3 8 8 5 9 6 3 *